For Mom & Dad

ATHENEUM BOOKS FOR YOUNG READERS · An imprint of Simon & Schuster Children's Publishing Division · 1230 Avenue of the Americas, New York, New York 10020 · Copyright © 2018 by Lucy Ruth Cummins · All rights reserved, including the right of reproduction in whole or in part in any form · ATHENEUM BOOKS FOR YOUNG READERS is a registered trademark of Simon & Schuster, Inc. Atheneum logo is a trademark of Simon & Schuster, Inc. · For information about special discounts for bulk purchases, please contact Simon & Schuster Special Sales at 1-866-506-1949 or business@simonandschuster.com. · The Simon & Schuster Speakers Bureau can bring authors to your live event. For more information or to book an event, contact the Simon & Schuster Speakers Bureau at 1-866-248-3049 or visit our website at www.simonspeakers.com. · Book design by Sonia Chaghatzbanian · The text for this book was set in Baskerville. · The illustrations for this book were rendered in gouache, pencil, ink, and brush marker. · Manufactured in China · 0518 SCP First Edition · 10 9 8 7 6 5 4 3 2 1 · Library of Congress Cataloging-in-Publication Data · Names: Cummins, Lucy Ruth, author, illustrator. · Title: Stumpkin / Lucy Ruth Cummins. · Description: First edition. | New York : Atheneum Books for Young Readers, [2018] | Summary: A stemless pumpkin that yearns to be a Halloween jack-o-lantern watches sadly as all of the other pumpkins in the shop are chosen. · Identifiers: LCCN 2017035040 (print) | LCCN 2017046311 (ebook) | ISBN 9781534413627 (alk. paper) | ISBN 9781534413634 (ebook) · Subjects: | CYAC: Pumpkin—Fiction. | Individuality—Fiction. | Jack-o-lanterns—Fiction. | Halloween—Fiction. · Classification: LCC PZ7.1.C86 (ebook) | LCC PZ7.1.C86 Stu 2018 (print) | DDC [E]—dc23 · LC record available at https://lccn.loc.gov/2017035040

Stumpkin

Lucy Ruth Cummins

Atheneum Books for Young Readers · New York · London · Toronto · Sydney · New Delhi

It was a few days before Halloween.

Outside a little shop in a big city, a shopkeeper

placed some pumpkins on the shelves.

A girl came and looked at the pumpkins.
When she was done, she picked one up and carried it away.

The other pumpkins worried after their friend.

But later they spotted him—

across the street and way up high.

He was a jack o'lantern!

Beneath his lovely stem he now had two triangle eyes,

a nose, and a giant toothy smile.

He had a new home.

A perch all to himself, high above the street.

What more could anyone want? thought the pumpkins.

They were *thrilled* for their friend.

And thrilled that they, too, might one day be jack o'lanterns.

They were all happily lost in thought, imagining themselves as jack o'lanterns, when one pumpkin realized something was very wrong.

Poor little pumpkin.

Poor little *stemless* pumpkin.

With just a stump, not a stem.

Poor little . . . *Stumpkin.*

Still there was *plenty* to like about Stumpkin.

He was a handsome pumpkin—as orange as a traffic cone.

He was as big as a basketball—and twice as round!

Stem-*schmem!*

Who knows?

Some people might even *prefer* a stemless pumpkin.

Days passed and more people came.

Some pumpkins left.

Some pumpkins stayed.

It wasn't yet Halloween.

There were still plenty of windows
that needed jack o'lanterns.

Who would be lucky enough to take home Stumpkin?

As orange as . . . an orange!

As big as a basketball!

Round!

He was very nearly the perfect pumpkin.

Very nearly. Truly!

The next day new people came.

And the shopkeeper's cat settled on Stumpkin's smooth top.

Then it happened—a brilliant baby chose Stumpkin!

Until a bad dog ruined it.

And the baby changed his mind.

Oh well, thought Stumpkin.

It was the day of Halloween.

There were still a few empty windows.

Two were left on the shopkeeper's shelf.

A boy came.

And when the boy left . . .

Stumpkin remained.

The gourd??
thought Stumpkin.
I guess that's that.

It was Halloween night, and the shop had closed.

The shopkeeper
scooped up
poor Stumpkin and
carried him off.

PUSH

Stumpkin wouldn't be getting a window.

And he wouldn't be getting a new home.

He already *had* a home.

And that made Stumpkin very, very happy.